Katie Morag
and the New Pier

High Farm

The Holiday House

Mrs Bayview's

The Lady A

The Redburn Bridge

The Village

THE ISLE of STRUAY

Grannie's

The Mainland

The Jetty

ISLE of STRUAY
SHOP & POST OFFICE

OBAN
TIMES
GET
YOUR COPY
HERE

The Shop & Post Office

To the old ways – and the new

KATIE MORAG AND THE NEW PIER
A RED FOX BOOK 978 1 849 41096 0

First published in Great Britain by The Bodley Head,
an imprint of Random House Children's Publishers UK

A Random House Group Company
The Bodley Head edition published 1993
Red Fox edition published 1997
This Red Fox edition published 2010

Red Fox Books are published by Random House Children's Publishers UK,
61–63 Uxbridge Road, London W5 5SA

www.randomhousechildrens.co.uk

Addresses for companies within The Random House Group Limited can be found at:
www.randomhouse.co.uk/offices.htm

THE RANDOM HOUSE GROUP Limited Reg. No. 954009

A CIP catalogue record for this book is available from the British Library.

Printed in China

Katie Morag
and the New Pier

Mairi Hedderwick

to the new pi

RED FOX

For months workmen had been building a new pier on the Isle of Struay. They were a cheery lot and lived in huts by the shore. They only complained when the weather got too bad to get on with the work; they felt homesick for their families and friends on the mainland.

They looked forward to the day the new pier would be finished. So did the islanders.

Katie Morag was especially excited about the new pier.

"The boat will be able to come to Struay THREE times a week instead of one," said her father, Mr McColl, the shopkeeper.

Mrs McColl, the postmistress, was delighted. She would have lots more mail deliveries to do.

MOUSE TRAPS
12 DOZEN

Post Office

OPEN

XMAS PARTY FUND

Isle of Struay

R.S.P.B. Slide Show Village Hall Wed. Evening

For Sale 6 Lobster Creels

Oban Times Buy your copy HERE

ISLE OF STRU

"Grandma Mainland will be able to come more often," said Neilly Beag.
"And she will be able to get away quicker," said Grannie Island, who was not
very sure about the new pier but saw that it had some advantages.

But for the most part Grannie Island was pessimistic.

"The old ways will be forgotten," she frowned. "The place will get too busy; there will be no more jaunts out in the ferryboat to the big boat in the Bay."

Grannie Island often manned the ferryboat on the days that the ferryman was ill or on holiday. "I'll miss that. And so will you, Katie Morag. And what will the ferryman do for a living?" Katie Morag hadn't thought about all that.

In the village people were saying it was time the old ways changed. They started to paint their windows and gates bright colours and tidy their gardens. Mrs Baxter said she was going to open up a Craft Shop. The Lady Artist, of course, was already making interesting things to sell in it.

On the other side of the Bay Mr MacMaster, the farmer, was very pleased. "I'll be able to send off eggs, milk and cheese to the mainland THREE times a week!"

"Ach well," sighed the ferryman, "I suppose I'll soon be redundant."

"What does that mean?" asked Katie Morag.

"No longer wanted," replied the ferryman as he and Katie Morag walked along the shore. Katie Morag nearly tripped over a large, blue, neatly coiled rope on the tideline.

"Finders keepers," said the ferryman. "That's the rule of the sea when something is washed up by the tide."

"Oh no – I'll give it to the ferryboat," declared Katie Morag.

"Have you been having chocolate cake again?" asked Mrs McColl crossly, as Katie Morag toyed with her tea that night. She had, but it wasn't the cake that was making Katie Morag sad. She tried to tell Mr and Mrs McColl all about the ferryman but her parents were not listening.

CALENDAR

BISTRO

Isle of Struay shop & P.O.
EXTENSION PLAN

"The pier will be finished by the spring, weather permitting," said Mrs McColl looking at the calendar.

Spring came but it did not come alone. It was accompanied by fearsome storms. One especially wet and windy day the foreman on the pier told the men to tie down the equipment and stop work. It was boring sitting in the huts waiting for the wild weather to end, so the workmen visited the islanders, and sat by their cosy fires and told stories about life on the mainland.

Jimmy and George were in the McColls' kitchen when the foreman burst in.
"The huts are floating out to sea!" he shouted.

Everyone rushed to the door and sure enough there was the new pier awash, but not a hut in sight save one that bobbed and bucked in the Bay. The rest had all sunk.

There was something else bobbing in the Bay. It was the ferryboat! Katie Morag could just make out the ferryman throwing a rope over the handle of the hut door. But as Grannie Island steered the ferryboat alongside, a huge wave lifted the rope off the handle and the hut started to drift out to sea again.

"Use my rope!" shouted Katie Morag at the top of her voice.

Grannie Island revved the boat close to the hut again and as she circled round it so went the strong blue rope.

Everyone cheered as the ferryboat towed the hut to the shore.

"What seamanship!" said the workmen. "What a rope!" said the ferryman, smiling at Katie Morag as he stepped out of the boat.

TOURIST INFORMATION

YOU ARE HERE

old pier
new pier
Island of Struay

"You can't sleep in that!" said the islanders as sodden mattresses and broken bits of furniture fell out of the hut door.

"You will just have to stay with us until the new pier is finished."

"Great!" thought Katie Morag. "Mainland stories every night!"

Next morning the storm had subsided and the men went back to work. The foreman said the ferryman could keep the hut for fire wood. He and the men thought it was just fine staying in the islanders' homes – much more comfortable than the huts.

Each workman boasted that his lodgings were the best but everyone had to agree that the ferryman's wife's chocolate cake was quite the most fabbydoo.

It was Easter and the new pier was finally completed. The boat came alongside laden with important people and visitors. And there was Grandma Mainland! The workmen shook hands with the islanders and said they would be back for their holidays. Nearly everyone wanted to book in at the ferryman's house and Katie Morag knew why.

"That's it, then," sighed Grannie Island as hordes of visitors meandered towards the village. "The end of the ferryboat and the old ways."

For Sale

Katie Morag Recipes

Menu

"No, it is not!" said Katie Morag taking her two grandmothers over to the ferryman's house. The hut was transformed: inside, a counter displayed several chocolate cakes and pots of tea. Grandma Mainland was first in the queue.

"After the visitors have had their tea, you and I and Katie Morag can take them out for a jaunt in the ferryboat, Grannie Island," suggested the ferryman.

"And you can tell them all about the old ways," said Katie Morag. Grannie Island smiled. The new pier was not going to be such a bad thing after all.

TEAS

Katie Morag
and the Dancing Class

High Farm

The Holiday House

The Lady Artis

Mrs Bayview's

The Redburn Bridge

The Village

Nurse's

Effie & Ronald the Road's

Mrs Baxter's

Neilly Beag's

The Ferryman's

TEAS

Grannie's

The Mainland

The New Pier

The Jetty

ISLE of STRUAY
SHOP & POST OFFICE

OBAN
TIMES
GET
YOUR COPY
HERE

BISTRO

TO THE
NEW PIER

CRAFTS

WELCOME

WEST
HIGHLAND
FREE PRESS

ORDER
NOW

LITTER

The Shop & Post Office

For Kirsty, Erika and Elizabeth, Stronvar and Port na Luing

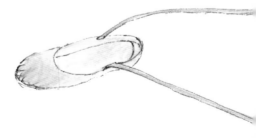

KATIE MORAG AND THE DANCING CLASS
A RED FOX BOOK 978 1 849 41085 4

First published in Great Britain by The Bodley Head,
an imprint of Random House Children's Publishers UK
A Random House Group Company

Bodley Head edition published 2007
Red Fox edition published 2008
This Red Fox edition published 2010

5 7 9 10 8 6 4

Red Fox Books are published by Random House Children's Publishers UK,
61–63 Uxbridge Road, London W5 5SA

www.randomhousechildrens.co.uk

Addresses for companies within The Random House Group Limited can be found at:
www.randomhouse.co.uk/offices.htm
THE RANDOM HOUSE GROUP Limited Reg. No. 954009

A CIP catalogue record for this book is available from the British Library.

Printed in China

Katie Morag
and the Dancing Class
Mairi Hedderwick

RED FOX

It was decided that it would be a good thing for the children on the Isle of Struay to have dancing lessons.

Agnes, Fay, Sasha and the Big Boy Cousins were keen to start, especially when they heard that Mrs Mackie would provide juice and biscuits at the end of each lesson.

The boys chose tap and the girls ballet. But Katie Morag McColl said she had better things to do on a Saturday morning – like getting a backy on her mother's Post Office bike or checking the lobster creels with Neilly Beag.

But Grannie Island said that ballet would be good for Katie Morag's co-ordination. Granma Mainland had already ordered pink pumps and a leotard from a dance shop on the Mainland. She was also sewing a frilly frou-frou skirt. She longed to see her granddaughter in a pretty outfit instead of that old jumper and skirt and those dreadful wellies.

Katie Morag loved her wellies.

She dreaded the thought of ballet lessons, but it had all been decided by the two grandmothers.

On the door sign:
I will tidy my bedroom tomorrow

On the first Saturday, Katie Morag reluctantly put on the leotard. Granma Mainland rushed into Katie Morag's bedroom waving a cloud of frills. The frou-frou skirt!

"Oh, no . . . !" thought Katie Morag. But, "Thank you very much, Granma Mainland," she said.

"Hurry up! Don't be late! There is to be a Dance Performance on Show Day! You will look SO pretty!" smiled Granma Mainland.

Katie Morag headed unwillingly towards the Village Hall. It was boat day and all the villagers were at the pier. But all was not silent and deserted at the last house in the Village. Nurse's gate was wide open and a flock of sheep were in her garden, baa-ing delightedly as they feasted on her early lettuces.

Katie Morag tried to chase them out but *every* time they came back in before she could close the gate.

After a long time, and a lot of shouting, which she enjoyed, Katie Morag finally got the sheep out and firmly shut the gate.

Katie Morag was late for ballet class . . .

On the second Saturday, Katie Morag decided to walk to the Village Hall along the shore. There had been a big storm in the night. She was on the lookout for anything interesting washed up on the tide line.

Once she had found a Frisbee which she gave to Liam for his birthday. And then there was the terrible time when she had been in a bad mood and had kicked her old teddy into the sea. She was so lucky to find him washed up two days later near Grannie Island's house.

This particular day, there was nothing special on the tide line –
but Katie Morag just *had* to keep on looking.

Katie Morag was *very* late for ballet class . . .

On the third Saturday, Flora Ann screamed all through breakfast. It being boat day, Katie Morag very kindly offered to stay with her until Mr and Mrs McColl collected the mail and supplies for the Shop and Post Office from the pier.

For once Katie Morag didn't mind having to look after her baby sister. Grannie Island was downstairs wiping the shelves in the Shop and completely forgot it was Dancing Class day. Katie Morag didn't remind her. The boat was an hour late in arriving.

Katie Morag was *extremely* late for ballet class.

SO LATE that she missed the whole class. Agnes, Fay and Sasha had already gone home. The Big Boy Cousins were putting on their tap shoes.

"What is it like to tap dance?" Katie Morag asked.

"It's like playing the drums with your feet," replied Hector, Archie, Dougal, Jamie and Murdo Iain, clacking the metal-studded toes and heels of their shoes on the floor.

WHAT A NOISE!

Katie Morag copied them with her wellies but the sound was like a wet fish flapping in the bottom of Neilly Beag's boat.

"You have to have the metal bits," laughed Jamie.

Mrs Mackie had been listening. "Would you like to come to tap, Katie Morag, instead of ballet? I am sure Granma Mainland would get you the shoes."

Katie Morag desperately wanted to say "Yes, please!" but she couldn't *possibly* ask Granma Mainland for more dancing shoes.

That night Katie Morag was staying over at Grannie Island's.

Wearily, she told Grannie Island the whole sad story.

"Take off your wellies," sighed Grannie Island sympathetically, "and have a rest by the fire."

Katie Morag looked at her wellies. "All they need are bits of metal . . ." she said forlornly.

Grannie Island suddenly started rummaging in a cupboard. She held up a pair of dusty leather boots. "My old tackety boots!"

"Silly Grannie!" scoffed Katie Morag, a bit rudely. "They are FAR TOO BIG!"

But Grannie Island was levering the metal tacks from their soles and hammering them onto the soles of Katie Morag's wellies.

PLEASE
LEAVE
KEY
WITH
MRS
BAYVIEW
—
THANKS
—

? HAVE YOU ?
SWITCHED
OFF **ALL**
LIGHTS
?
?

STRUAY VILLAGE HALL NOTICES

WOODWORK THURSDAYS

PIGLETS for SALE

BALLET CLASS 10 AM SATS.

TAP CLASS 11 AM SATS

R.N.L.I. DANCE FRID. 10 PM

SHOW COMMITTEE MEETING URGENT

PILATES

On the fourth Saturday, on the dot of 11 o'clock, Katie Morag was the first at the door of the Hall. Mrs Mackie said not a word about the rather unusual tap shoes.

"What are you like, Katie Morag?" the Big Boy Cousins groaned.

But Jamie laughed. "She's like she is. She's Katie Morag!"

Katie Morag worked really hard to catch up on her cousins.
Rehearsals had already started for the Dance Performance on Show Day.
Mrs Mackie made them practise their routine over and over again.

On the evening of the Dance Performance,
the islanders packed into the Village Hall.
The two grandmothers were in the front row;
Granma Mainland dressed up in all her finery,
looking forward to seeing Katie Morag in *her* finery . . .

Granma Mainland was so disappointed when she saw Katie Morag wearing that old jumper and skirt and those dreadful wellies – *on the stage!*

But when Katie Morag danced perfectly in time with the Big Boy Cousins and even did a solo turn in her tackety wellies, Granma Mainland had to admit that she was extremely impressed.

Katie Morag was equally impressed by the ballet performance. Agnes was Aladdin, in a blue satin bolero and baggy trousers, and Sasha was Princess Jasmine in veils of purple silk. Fay performed high wild kicks as the Genie coming out of the lamp.

At the end of the wonderful evening, the Lady Artist thanked Mrs Mackie for all her hard work and gave her a bouquet of flowers specially ordered from the Mainland.

"And I would like to thank all the dancers who worked so very hard, too," Mrs Mackie replied. "Katie Morag worked the hardest of them all!"

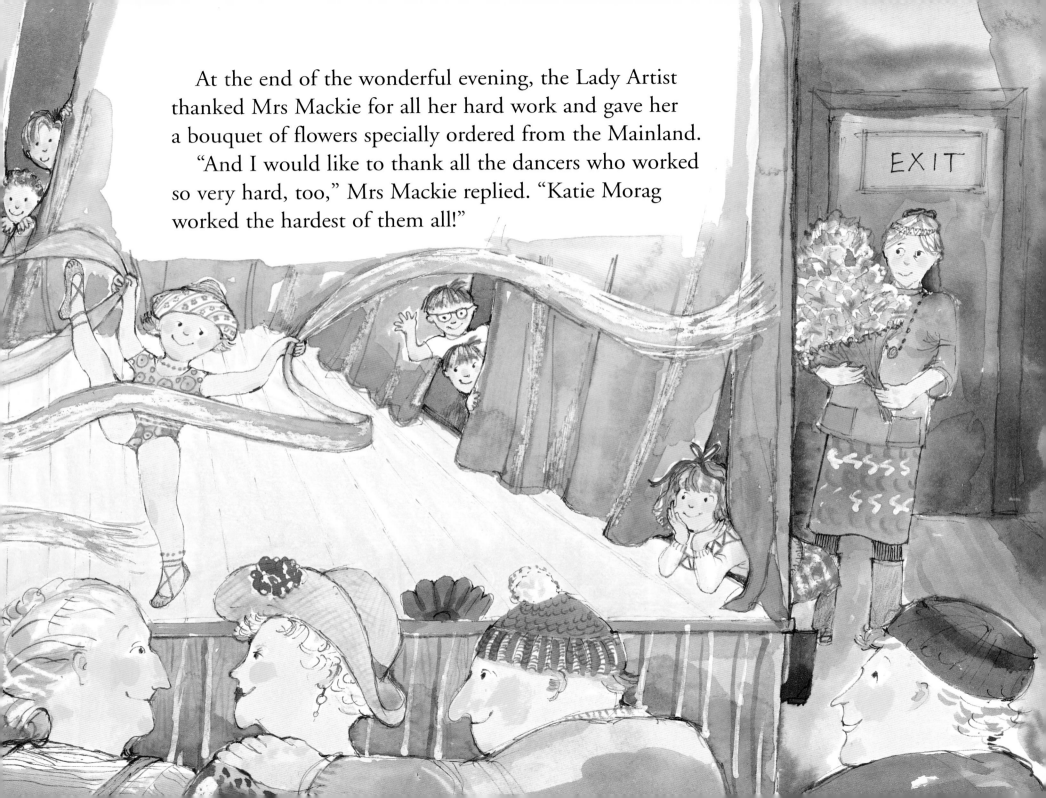

Afterwards, Katie Morag apologized to Granma Mainland for not telling her about missing ballet lessons and how she really liked tap dancing.

Then she said, "But Granma Mainland, I think I would like to go to both classes next year . . ."

Granma Mainland smiled her forgiveness. Maybe she would see Katie Morag in that frilly frou-frou skirt one day, after all.

Miss McColl Isle of Struay

URGENT

WELLIES (Black)
SIZE: 1/33

"And, look," said Katie Morag brightly, "the ballet shoes I didn't use this year won't be wasted. They will make cosy liners for my wellies in the winter!"

Join Katie Morag on more adventures!

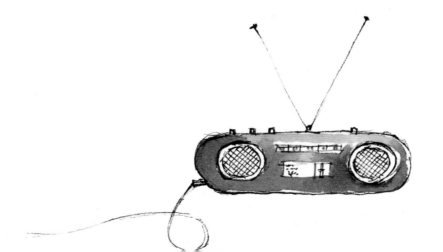